Homage to Cosmo

First published 1993
by Walker Books Ltd, 87 Vauxhall Walk
London SE11 5HJ

© 1993 Camilla Ashforth

This book had been typeset in Garamond.

Printed and bound in Italy by L.E.G.O., Vicenza

British Library Cataloguing in Publication Data
A catalogue record for this title is available
from the British Library.

ISBN 0-7445-2578-0

CALAMITY

Camilla Ashforth

WALKER BOOKS
LONDON

James and Horatio were
building a tower.
"One, two, three," said James
as he balanced the blocks.
"Seven, four," added Horatio.

"HEE-HAW!"

BUMP!

Something crashed into the Useful
Box and sent everything flying.

"What was that?" asked Horatio.
"It's a calamity," said James,
looking at the mess.
"What were you doing, Calamity?"
asked Horatio.
"Racing," Calamity said. "And I won."

"Can I race?" asked Horatio.
"Find yourself a jockey," Calamity said.
"Here's mine." She turned round.
But that's a bobbin, thought James.
He started to tidy up.

Horatio looked for a jockey.
I like this one, he thought.
It was James's clock.
"Are you ready?" asked Calamity.
They waited a moment.

"One, two, three, go!" Calamity
called. She hurtled round the
Useful Box. Twice.

Horatio tried to move his jockey.

He pushed it

and pulled it.

Then he rolled
it over.

His jockey would not budge.

Calamity screeched to a halt.

"Hee-haw! I won!" she bellowed.

"Let's race again."

James turned round.

He picked up Horatio's jockey.

"That's my clock," said James and he put it in his Useful Box.

Horatio looked for another jockey.

"One, two, three, go!" Calamity called.
She galloped very fast.
Backwards and forwards.

Horatio looked around.
I'll go this way, he thought, and
he set off with his new jockey.

"Hee-haw! Won again!" cried
Calamity, stopping suddenly.
Horatio looked puzzled.
"One more race," Calamity said.
"I'm good at this."

"James," whispered Horatio, "can you help me win this time?"

"What you need is a race track," said James. "I'll make you one."

"This block is the start," he said.

"And this string is the finishing line.
Ready, steady, go!"

Calamity thundered off.
She was going the wrong way.

Horatio headed for the finishing line
as fast as he could.

Calamity turned in a circle and
headed back towards James.

"Stop!" James cried.

As Horatio crossed the line, Calamity collided with the Useful Box.
CRASH!

"That was a good race. Who won?" asked Calamity.
"I think you both did," James said, and squeezed Horatio tight.